MEET THE FRAGGLES

By Michaela Muntean
Pictures by Barbara Lanza

Muppet Press
Holt, Rinehart and Winston
NEW YORK

Published by Holt, Rinehart and Winston,
383 Madison Avenue, New York, New York 10017.

Library of Congress Cataloging in Publication Data
Muntean, Michaela.
Meet the Fraggles.
Summary: Introduces Doozers, Fraggles, and Gorgs and
offers advice on how to handle them as houseguests.
(It would be best *not* to let a Gorg in your house.)
1. Children's stories, American.   [1. Puppets—Fic-
tion]   I. Lanza, Barbara, ill.   II. Title.
PZ7.M929Me   1985   [E]   84-19182

ISBN: 0-03-003263-6
First Edition
Printed in the United States of America
1 3 5 7 9 10 8 6 4 2

ISBN 0-03-003263-6

HAVE you ever wondered what you would do if a Doozer, a Fraggle, or a Gorg ever came to visit you? Where would they sleep? What would they eat?

Well, put your wonders and worries aside, for here is the Official Guide to Entertaining Doozers, Fraggles, and Gorgs!

PART I
DOOZERS

Doozers, as everyone knows, are quite small. They stand six inches high, which is about as tall as a medium-sized banana.

Doozers are a pale, pear-green color and have rather chubby, pear-shaped bodies.

Doozers are hard-working, quiet, and thoughtful. They are very polite. Doozers always remember to say, "Excuse me," to send thank-you notes, and to return their library books on time.

A Doozer would make a perfect houseguest, which is good to know in case you ever find a Doozer on your doorstep. You would have only a few small problems, but they are very small problems: where to put, what to feed, and how to entertain your Doozer-size guest.

Sleeping

Doozers like cozy, snug-as-a-bug places to sleep.

Bathing

Sinks are probably safest, but be sure the drain is closed!

Feeding

Small food is recommended. Peas or raisins would be fine; whole pineapples would not.

Traveling

You can tuck a Doozer in almost any comfortable little place. There is always room for a Doozer, so don't leave home without one!

Sight-seeing with Your Doozer Guest

Doozers would probably enjoy a trip to a museum, but a tour of a construction site, road work, or a factory would be the most exciting for your Doozer guest.

Sports

All work and no play makes a dull Doozer. Doozers are
always ready to have a little fun after a hard day's work.

Warning: Do not be surprised if you begin to discover construction sites in and around your home while a Doozer is visiting.

PART II
FRAGGLES

FRAGGLES are three times taller than Doozers and about thirty times noisier. If a Fraggle should drop in on you, find a park, a playground, or a place to swim nearby, because Fraggles need plenty of room to run, skip, hop, jump, dance, and swim.

Fraggle-size spaces are only a medium-size problem,
and you should not have too much trouble finding
a place to put a Fraggle guest.

Sleeping

Fraggle-size sleeping spaces should be dark and quiet.
If you do not happen to live in a cave, any one of these
places will do.

Bathing

A word of caution: Fraggles love water and will tend to jump in whenever they can. This can sometimes be embarrassing.

Feeding

Fraggles like radishes best of all, but turnips, spinach, beans, and pickles also make a good Fraggle feast.

You may quickly run out of radish recipes, so here are a few ideas you may find helpful:

Interesting Radish Recipes:

radish cake

sliced radishes on toast

radish roast

stuffed radishes

radish shish kebab

radish sundae

Traveling

Fraggles have lots of energy and they are always ready to go anywhere, anytime.

Sight-seeing with Your Fraggle Guest

Although Fraggles love art and music, parades, carnivals, and amusement parks would probably be the most interesting.

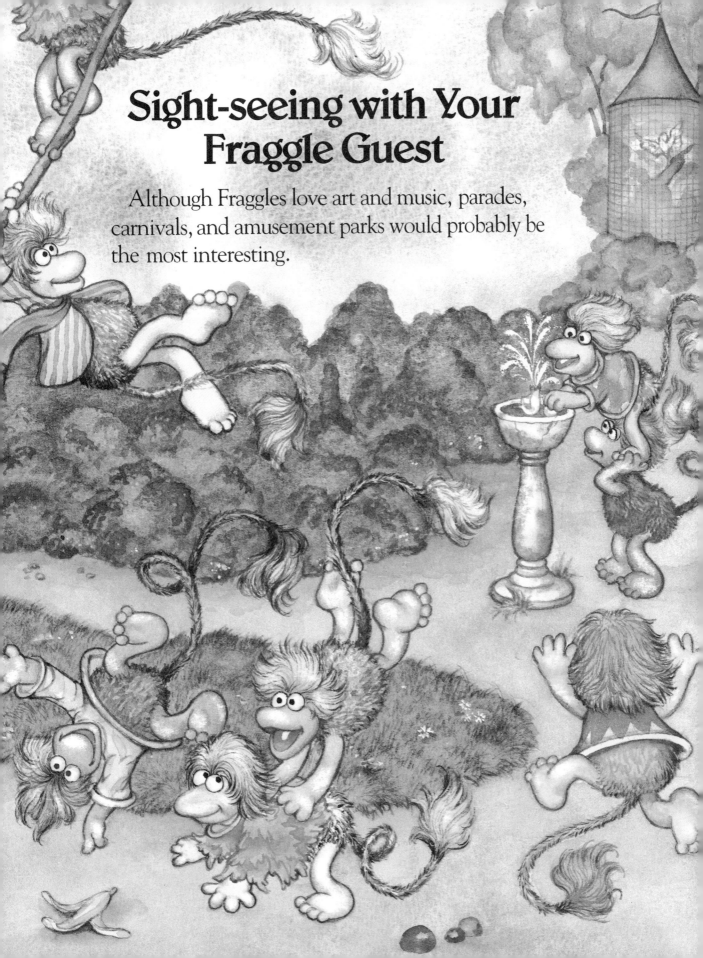

Sports

Almost anything you can think of is a game to a Fraggle.
Trying on hats is a favorite pastime.

Warning: Do not be surprised if you discover that your Fraggle guest spends a lot of time in the basement of your house or under the sink in your kitchen. Fraggles like dark places filled with plenty of plumbing.

PART III
GORGS

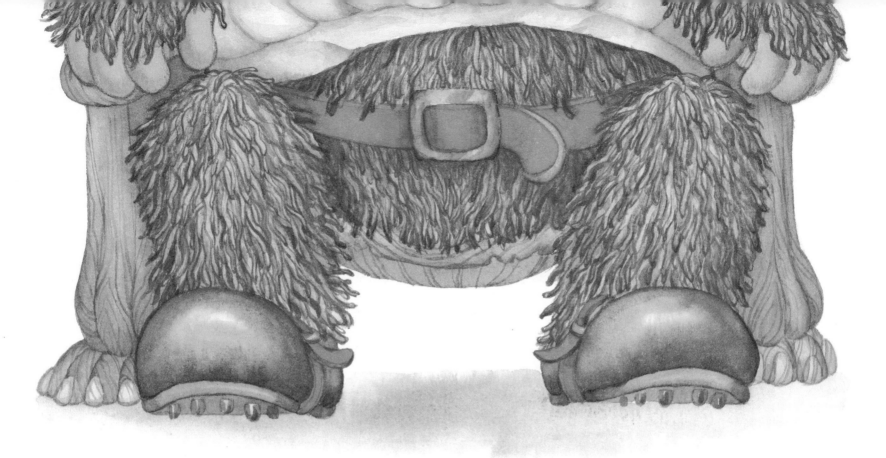

Unless you have a soft heart (or a soft head), my advice is *do not* under any circumstances, ever, ever, *ever* let a Gorg in your house. First of all, a Gorg would probably not even fit in your house. Well, maybe his big toe would, and *maybe* if you lived in a castle, or happened to have a very large, very empty barn, you *might* be able to squeeze a Gorg inside.

As you can see, a Gorg is Big. And when I say big, I mean Big with a capital B. A Gorg is as tall as a giraffe-and-a-half and as fat as two elephants put together.

Feeding

To feed a Gorg guest, you would have to buy truckloads of food, and that would still probably not be enough.

Traveling

Forget about going anywhere! A moving van or a dump truck would be too small to haul a Gorg! Sight-seeing would also be out—everyone would run if they saw you first!

To add to everything else, a Gorg is very lazy. Not only will he take up a lot of room, eat a lot of food, make a whole lot of mess, and probably squish, squash, or smash everything in sight, but he won't clean up any of it when he leaves.

Warning: It would be best for all involved if you remain firmly rude and do not answer the door if a Gorg should come calling.

So keep this book on hand, and you will always be ready if a Doozer or a Fraggle or even a Gorg comes to visit you!